Noah and his wife think a flood might be coming, so they have built a big boat called the Ark. They are sailing around the world to rescue the animals before it starts to rain.

Let's all go on an animal adventure!

Reading Consultant: Prue Goodwin, Lecturer in literacy and children's books

ORCHARD BOOKS
338 Euston Road, London NW1 3BH
Orchard Books Australia
Level 17/207 Kent Street, Sydney, NSW 2000

First published in 2011
First paperback publication in 2012

ISBN 978 1 40830 557 7 (hardback)
ISBN 978 1 40830 565 2 (paperback)

A CIP catalogue record for this book is available from the British Library.

1 3 5 7 9 10 8 6 4 2 (hardback)
1 3 5 7 9 10 8 6 4 2 (paperback)

Printed in China

Orchard Books is a division of Hachette Children's Books, an Hachette UK company.

Kung Fu Kangaroos!

Written by Sally Grindley
Illustrated by Alex Paterson

“Land ahoy!” cried Noah.

“At last!” said Mrs Noah.

“We’ve been at sea

for days.”

"The sign says Australia," said Noah.

"I wonder which animals we'll

find there."

Noah picked up their *Big Book of Animals.*

"Kangaroos!" he said. "It says they hop and like to box."

"You had better watch out," smiled Mrs Noah. "They might punch you on the nose!"

"Oh dear!" said Noah.

They reached the shore and anchored the Ark. Noah went inside to change. He also collected a pair of boxing gloves and a pogo stick.

"Now I feel like a kangaroo!" he said.

"You don't look like one!" laughed Mrs Noah.

Noah lowered the gangplank and stepped onto the beach. He jumped onto the pogo stick and set off across the sand.

He bounced over the dry grass.

He bounced through the tall trees.

He bounced across the wide stream.

"This is fun!" Noah cried. Just then, he fell off and landed in a prickly bush. "Now I feel like a hedgehog," he moaned.

Noah pulled the prickles from his knees. Suddenly, he heard a noise. "What was that?" he whispered.

He peered round the bush. A large animal was standing on the dusty ground close by, scratching its ear. "It's a kangaroo!" cried Noah.

Then another kangaroo came
bounding over.

“Two kangaroos!” said Noah.

“I wonder if they’re going to box?”

The kangaroos began to eat leaves from the bush. Soon, they spotted Noah.

“Hello,” called Noah, waving. “We make very tasty meals on my Ark,” he said. “Would you like to come and try them?”

Noah stepped out from behind the bush. "My, you have got big feet," he said to the kangaroos.

The first kangaroo biffed him on the ear.

The other kangaroo biffed him on the other ear.

"Ouch!" cried Noah. "I didn't mean to be rude!"

Noah put on his boxing gloves. “Let’s have a proper match, then,” he said.

He started to skip around, biffing the air with his fists.

The kangaroos started to skip around, too.

“Stand still!” said Noah. “You’re too quick!”

The first kangaroo hopped towards Noah, threw a punch and biffed him on the nose. Noah fell to the ground.

Just then, Mrs Noah arrived on a pogo stick of her own. On her back was a large sack.

"It looks like you're no match for a boxing kangaroo, Noah!" she laughed.

Noah groaned. Mrs Noah helped him to his feet.

"My nose is squashed," he grumbled.

"Silly Noah," smiled Mrs Noah.

Mrs Noah opened the sack she was carrying. It was full of rich, green grass.

The kangaroos stood up on their hind legs and clucked eagerly.

“Follow me,” laughed Mrs Noah.

“There’s plenty more grass on our Ark.

Come on, Noah, off we go.”

She hopped back onto her pogo stick.

Noah and the kangaroos followed her.

They bounced across the wide stream.

They bounced through the tall trees.

They bounced over the dry grass.

"Now, Noah," said Mrs Noah, when they reached the Ark. "Would you like a bowl of grass like your kangaroo friends? Or how about a nice box of chocolates?"

She hooted with laughter.

"Do you get it, Noah? A *box* of chocolates? Ha!"

SALLY GRINDLEY • ALEX PATERSON

Crazy Chameleons!	978 1 40830 562 1
Giant Giraffes!	978 1 40830 563 8
Too-slow Tortoises!	978 1 40830 564 5
Kung Fu Kangaroos!	978 1 40830 565 2
Playful Penguins!	978 1 40830 566 9
Pesky Sharks!	978 1 40830 567 6
Cheeky Chimpanzees!	978 1 40830 568 3
Hungry Bears!	978 1 40830 569 0

All priced at £4.99